The Great Treefle Hunt

We need to turn the magic on,
We need to save the day, come on!

BANTAM
BOOKS

TREE FU TOM: THE GREAT TREEFLE HUNT

A BANTAM BOOK 978 0 857 51158 4
First published in Great Britain by Bantam, an imprint of Random House Children's Publishers UK
A Random House Group Company.

This edition published 2013

1 3 5 7 9 10 8 6 4 2

Tree Fu Tom created by Daniel Bays.
Based on the episode 'Treefle Tom', written by John Loy.
TREE FU TOM word and device marks are trade marks of the British Broadcasting
Corporation and FremantleMedia Enterprises and are used under licence. TREE FU TOM device
marks © BBC and FremantleMedia Enterprises MMX. The "BBC" word mark and logo are trade
marks of the British Broadcasting Corporation and are used under licence. BBC Logo © BBC 1996.
Licensed by FremantleMedia Enterprises.

Set in Trebuchet MS Regular.

Bantam Books are published by Random House Children's Publishers UK,
61-63 Uxbridge Road, London W5 5SA

www.**randomhousechildrens**.co.uk

Addresses for companies within The Random House Group Limited can be found at:
www.randomhouse.co.uk/offices.htm

THE RANDOM HOUSE GROUP Limited Reg. No. 954009

A CIP catalogue record for this book is available from the British Library.

Printed in China

The Random House Group Limited supports the Forest Stewardship Council® (FSC®), the leading
international forest-certification organization. Our books carrying the FSC label are printed
on FSC®-certified paper. FSC is the only forest certification scheme supported by the leading
environmental organizations, including Greenpeace. Our paper procurement policy can be found
at www.randomhouse.co.uk/environment

The Great Treefle Hunt

Tom cheered. He and Twigs were playing an exciting game of Squizzle against Ariela, Zigzoo and Squirmtum.

"Yes!" shouted Tom, leaping up to catch the Squizzle in one hand. Three wingseeds were sent spinning to the bottom of their posts.

Twigs swooped down to give Tom a high-five. "Nice one!" he grinned. "We are the Squizzle kings!"

"Tom and Twigs win," laughed Ariela.

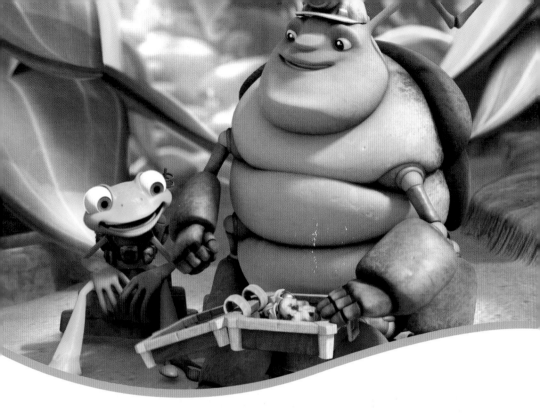

The friends sat down to enjoy the sunshine.

Squirmtum opened his lunch box. Five sweet

Trillicakes were waiting inside.

"I'm up for a Trillicake!" beamed Twigs.

"Me too!" agreed

the others.

Teabiscuit bounded over.
He began to snuffle in
the bushes.
"What's got him so excited?"
asked Tom.
Ariela looked in Teabiscuit's mouth.
There was a glowing fruit inside.

Zigzoo took the
fruit and held it up in the air.
"It's a Treefle!" he gasped.
"What's a Treefle?" asked Tom.
 "Only the tastiest treat in all of Treetopolis!"
replied Ariela.

Ariela explained that Treefles were magical
and very rare. They tasted yummy!
"There's no way they're better than my
mum's apple crumble," thought Tom.
Ariela smiled. "Try it and see."

Tom took a bite
of the Treefle.
"Mmm," he
agreed. "That
is good."
Ariela was right.
Treefles really were the
tastiest treat in Treetopolis!

Everybody shared the
Treefle, but one bite
just wasn't enough.
"I want more,"
decided Squirmtum.
"Me too!"
added Tom.
"Me three!" chipped
in Twigs.

Finding more Treefles

wasn't going to be easy.

They grew in the shadows, hidden away,

for one day only.

"Today must be the day!" cried Ariela.

"Let's split up and share the Treefles we find,"

replied Tom.

The Treefle search was on, but
only Ariela seemed to be finding any.
"Yeeha!" she cried, riding on Teabiscuit's back.
Teabiscuit snuffled through the bushes, then
rooted out another Treefle.
"I'll need a magic spell to sniff out Treefles like
Teabiscuit," decided Tom.

"But first I need to do
the moves to turn my magic powers on."

TIME FOR TREE FU!

Slide to the side, and jump right back!
Hold your hands up high...
Touch your nose.
Now make a pose!
Touch your knees,
and run with me!

"Look!" said Tom.
"The sapstone
in my belt is
glowing. Moving
turned the
magic on!"

Tom wanted to sniff out
Treefles. He cast a SUPER
SMELL spell on himself.
A green pong suddenly filled
the air around him.
"Yuck!" gasped Twigs.
Ariela snorted. "You've made yourself smell!
You should have done a spell to smell well."
Tom turned the SUPER SMELL magic off.

Zigzoo drove his wagon into the clearing.

He had a new invention to show his friends.

"This is my Super Seek-a-matic!" he cried.

"It will seek out Treefles wherever they are."

Zigzoo pushed the power level up one notch.

The Super Seek-a-matic chugged forward. A big tube on the front sucked up seeds and leaves. As it sniffed around, it pulled Zigzoo's wagon along.

The Super Seek-a-matic pushed past Teabiscuit. A Treefle whizzed up the sucking tube and into the collecting bag. The machine was an even better Treefle sniffer than Teabiscuit! Zigzoo opened a hatch and pulled out the Treefle.

Everybody wanted
more. One by one,
they pushed the
Super Seek-a-matic's
power lever up.
"More power!"
shouted Twigs.

"More Treefles!" added Tom.
"Turn it up!" yelled Squirmtum.

"NO!" cried Zigzoo.
The Super Seek-a-matic was out of control!

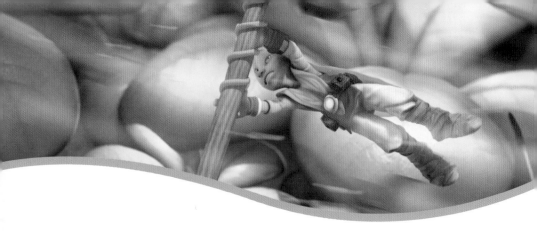

Zigzoo's machine stirred up a whirlwind.

"We've turned it up too high," yelled Tom.

The friends clung onto branches, but Twigs was

sucked into the Super Seek-a-matic!

Tom needed Big World Magic to squeeze the

sniffing tube shut and get Twigs out.

"It's time to do the SUPER SQUEEZE spell," he said.

TREE FU GO!

Arms up in the air!
Spread your fingers, squeeze one hand,
squeeze your other hand and
squeeze your hands together.
Now clap and say
'Super Squeeze'!

The magic worked! The
Seek-a-matic stopped. Twigs popped
his head out of the hatch. Ariela gasped.
"He's eating the Treefles!"

Tom searched the collecting bag. He found
one last Treefle and took a big bite.
"Hey!" yelled Squirmtum, snatching it from Tom.
Before he could eat the lot, Ariela grabbed the
fruit. Then Zigzoo barged in to finish it off.

"We were supposed to share!" moaned Twigs.

"No way," snapped Ariela. "I'm not sharing with
you anymore!"

"I'm not sharing with you either," he shouted back.

Everyone began to argue.

"I can find my own Treefles," sniffed Squirmtum.

Tom shook his head. "Not if I beat you there first..."

Tom, Ariela, Squirmtum, Twigs and Zigzoo headed off in different directions. Nobody wanted to work together now.

Ariela rooted around under a plant and pulled out a... Treefle!
"This one's mine!" she beamed.
"No!" cried Twigs. "It's mine!"
He reached for the Treefle but missed, landing on the ground with a noisy bump!

Tom wasn't doing much better.

"Come on," he urged, pulling up a large Treefle.

"Yes!"

SNIFF! SNIFF!

Teabiscuit skidded up behind Tom. He was after

Treefles, too! He snorted loudly. Tom dropped

his Treefles and ran.

Zigzoo searched around his boat.

"Where are you lovely... Treefles!" he cried,

spotting some.

Squirmtum had seen the Treefles, too. Both dived

to get them, but Twigs swooped in and took the lot.

BANG!

Twigs flew straight into

the boat and dropped

all his Treefles!

Zigzoo caught the falling Treefles, but Tom used a SUPER GRAB spell to take them.

"Don't count your Treefles before they're snatched!" he shouted. He flew off into the Sap Caverns with his arms full.

Twigs, Zigzoo, Ariela and Squirmtum all chased after Tom.

"Come back!" shouted Zigzoo.

"Give me back those Treefles!" added Ariela.

Tom flew into a cavern. He looked up.

"Wow!" he gasped.

Tom rubbed his eyes. The cavern was full of plump, golden Treefles!

The others ran into the cave, too.

Everyone started pulling
Treefles out of the walls.
Nobody talked. Nobody
shared. They

were too busy

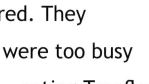

eating Treefles.

"What was that?" asked Tom.

The cavern rumbled and shook.

Without Treefles to hold it

together, the walls were cracking!

Pieces of wall and ceiling
fell all around the greedy
Treefle hunters.

BOOM!

The cavern entrance collapsed!

"We're trapped!" gasped Squirmtum.

"If we want to get out of here," realised
Tom, "we've got to put our Treefles down and
work together!"
Ariela wasn't sure. She didn't trust her friends
not to steal her Treefles.
"Only if you go first!" she shouted.

Tom looked at the ceiling. It was going to
fall soon!
 "OK," he agreed. He decided to drop his
Treefles. One by one, each of his friends
dropped their Treefles, too.

The friends tried to lift the rocks away from the entrance. It was nearly too late – the ceiling was falling down!

"We'll have to use Big World Magic to protect everyone," decided Tom.

It was time for the GIANT SHIELD spell.

TREE FU GO!

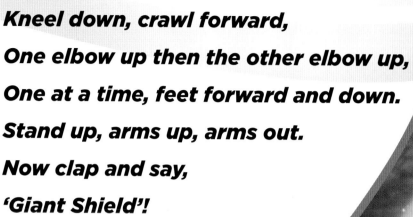

Kneel down, crawl forward,
One elbow up then the other elbow up,
One at a time, feet forward and down.
Stand up, arms up, arms out.
Now clap and say,
'Giant Shield'!

A golden shield
appeared above Tom
and his friends.
Boulders bounced
off it.
"I can't hold
it for long!"
warned Tom,
"work fast!"

The friends hurried to clear a way out. They each squeezed out of the cavern. Tom dived out too, just as the ceiling fell in. They'd all made it! "There go the Treefles," sighed Twigs. Squirmtum smiled and lifted up his helmet.

He'd saved one last Treefle.

"Do you want to share it?" he offered.

The friends each took turns to have a bite.
"One Treefle shared together tastes so much
better than a whole load of them eaten on your
own," realised Tom.

Everybody agreed.

"I'm sorry I took your Treefles everyone," said Tom.

"I'm sorry, too," replied Twigs.

Squirmtum and Zigzoo nodded their heads.

"Sorry, guys," smiled Ariela. "Being greedy only brings trouble."

BLURP -BUP- BLURP!

Twigs felt his tummy wibble.

"Yes," he laughed, "tummy trouble!"